"Goodnight Volunteers"

By Samantha Hawthorne

ISBN: 979-8-6100-3848-3

Goodnight

Volunteers

There's a school that's known for excellence.

It's better than all the rest.

Volunteers never falter.

Tennessee is the best!

Volunteers love to win, they never lose it.

It's an honor and a privilege,
to be a Tennessee student.

They study to be doctors and lawyers,

musicians, and dancers.

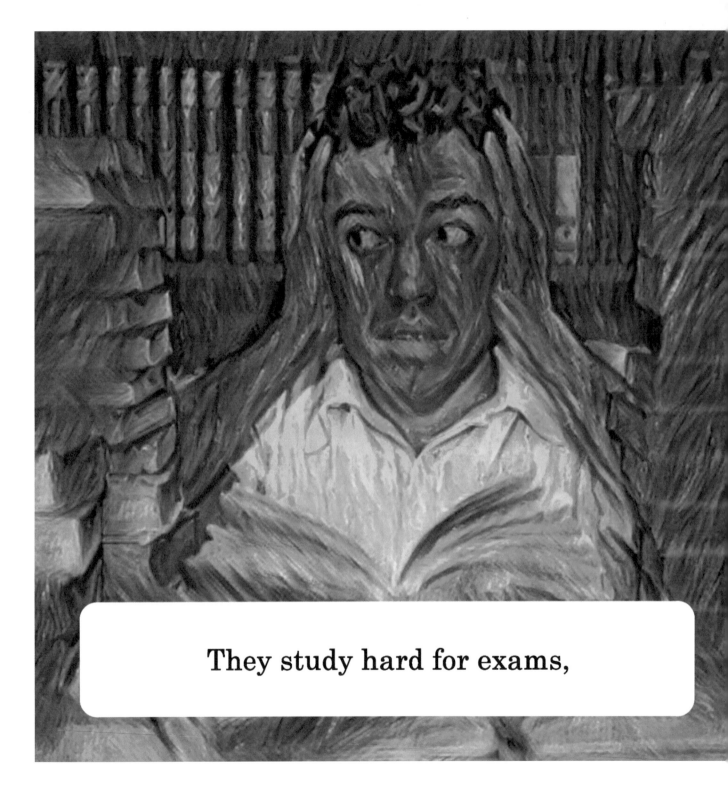

They study hard for exams,

to learn all the answers.

But now, it's getting late.

It's time to say goodnight.

Goodnight, beautiful campus.

Goodnight, incoming freshmen.

Goodnight, Neyland Stadium.

Goodnight, student section.

Goodnight, homework.

Goodnight, tests.

Goodnight, Tennessee...

you are the best!

Goodnight, Mom. Goodnight, Dad.

One day, I too...

will be a Tennessee grad.

Goodnight, Volunteers!

Made in the USA
Columbia, SC
27 August 2024

41239347R00015